Tadpoles Tales

Old Man Kangaroo

Retold by Robert James

Illustrated by Pedro Penizzotto

First published in 2010 by
Franklin Watts
338 Euston Road
London
NW1 3BH

Franklin Watts Australia
Level 17/207 Kent Street
Sydney
NSW 2000

Text © Franklin Watts 2010
Illustration © Pedro Penizzotto 2010

ISBN 978 0 7496 9407 4 (hbk)
ISBN 978 0 7496 9413 5 (pbk)

Series Editor: Jackie Hamley
Series Advisor: Catherine Glavina
Series Designer: Peter Scoulding

Printed in China

Franklin Watts is a division of
Hachette Children's Books,
an Hachette UK company.
www.hachette.co.uk

This Just So story is
based on a tale written
by an author called
Rudyard Kipling over
a hundred years ago.

Just So stories give fun
ideas for why different
animals are like they are.

Long ago, Kangaroo
had four short legs.

He thought he was the best animal in the world.

Kangaroo went to see the desert god.

"Make me different from all the other animals!" he demanded.

"Of course," agreed the desert god. "Chase him, Dingo!"

Dingo chased
Kangaroo right
across the desert.

He chased Kangaroo
right over the
mountains.

Kangaroo came to a wide river.

He stood up on his back
legs and hopped across.

Kangaroo kept hopping.

His back legs got stronger and stronger.

Back in the desert, the desert god laughed.

"Now you are different from the other animals, Kangaroo!"

Puzzle Time!

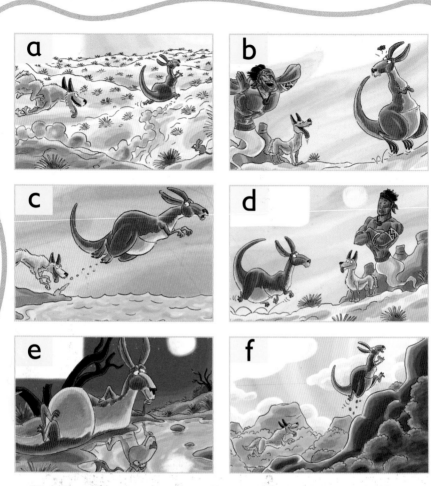

Put these pictures in the right order and tell the story!

vain

clever

wise

proud

Which words describe Kangaroo
and which describe
the desert god?

Turn over for answers!

Notes for adults

TADPOLES are structured to provide support for newly independent readers. The stories may also be used by adults for sharing with young children.

Starting to read alone can be daunting. **TADPOLES** help by providing visual support and repeating words and phrases. These books will both develop confidence and encourage reading and rereading for pleasure.

If you are reading this book with a child, here are a few suggestions:

1. Make reading fun! Choose a time to read when you and the child are relaxed and have time to share the story.
2. Talk about the story before you start reading. Look at the cover and the blurb. What might the story be about? Why might the child like it?
3. Encourage the child to retell the story, using the jumbled picture puzzle as a starting point. Extend vocabulary with the matching words to characters puzzle.
4. Talk about how the story has fun with how different animals look, and see if you can think of other animals and why they might look the way they do.
5. Give praise! Remember that small mistakes need not always be corrected.

Answers

Here is the correct order:

1. e 2. d 3. a 4. f 5. c 6. b

Words to describe Kangaroo:
proud, vain

Words to describe
the desert god:
clever, wise